Lenny and Mel's SUMMER VACATION

STORY AND PICTURES BY

ERIK P. KRAFT

Simon & Schuster Books for Young Readers

New York   London   Toronto   Sydney   Singapore

SIMON & SCHUSTER BOOKS FOR YOUNG READERS
An imprint of Simon & Schuster Children's Publishing Division
1230 Avenue of the Americas, New York, New York 10020

Book design by Greg Stadnyk
The text for this book is set in Berkeley Book.
The illustrations are rendered in pen and ink.
Manufactured in the United States of America
10 9 8 7 6 5 4 3 2 1

Library of Congress Cataloging-in-Publication Data
Kraft, Erik.
p. cm.
Summary: Twin brothers Lenny and Mel spend an uneventful summer that climaxes with a lackluster vacation.
ISBN 0-689-85108-1 (hardcover)
[1. Twins—Fiction. 2. Brothers—Fiction. 3. Summer—Fiction. 4. Vacations—Fiction.] I. Title.
PZ7.K85843 Lg 2003
[Fic]—dc21
2002006919

* first *
edition

To Frank and Renie

Contents

Best Day Ever

That day is like no other. The sun seems sunnier, the birds are not all pigeons, hot dogs are plumper, and real dogs don't smell quite as bad when they get wet.

It was the first day of summer vacation.

"This is the best," said Lenny.

"You bet," said Mel.

They were in the living room. Mel was lying on the couch. Lenny was lying on the floor. It was nine A.M. and they weren't at school.

"I could do this all day," said Lenny.

"I could do this all summer," said Mel.

The boys' father walked into the room. "So

what are the big plans for vacation?" he asked.

"This," said Lenny, not moving.

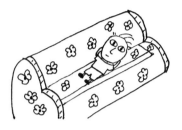  

"That's not very exciting," said their father.

"It's a free country," said Mel.

"Well, you're going to get bored very quickly if you don't think of stuff to do."

"We haven't done this since last summer," said Lenny.

"Too bad camp wouldn't take you back," said their father. "They'd have plenty for you to do."

"Aren't you late for work?" asked Mel.

Their father looked at the clock. "Eegah!" he shouted, and he bolted out the door.

"Wait! Your lunch!" shouted their mother, and she ran after him, just like every other morning.

"No rushing around for us," said Lenny.

"None at all," said Mel.

And they hunkered down for a day of doing what they were doing: nothing.

"Ugh, why'd he have to mention camp?" said Lenny. "This beats camp any day."

"You bet," said Mel. "No one around to steal your pudding when you're not looking."

"None of that smelly crud in the tire swing," said Lenny.

"That stuff that was full of mosquitoes?" asked Mel.

"That's the stuff," said Lenny. "And no having to make those awful Pioneer Biscuits."

"Those things were hard," said Mel. "I almost broke a tooth."

"I think I still have a bruise from where you threw yours at me," said Lenny.

"Oh," said Mel. "Sorry about that."

"Enough talk," said Lenny. "We're on vacation."

"Oh, right," said Mel.

Animal Town

"Okay, kids," said their mother. "No more sitting around being bored. Let's go to Animal Town."

"Eh," said Mel from the couch.

"Umf," said Lenny from the floor.

"Come on!" she said. "You boys love animals."

"Is Animal Town a zoo?" asked Mel.

"It's different from a zoo," said their mother.

"Yeah, no elephants," said Lenny.

"Zoos can be zoos without elephants," said Mel. "They just need weird stuff. Do they have wombats?"

"No," said their mother.

"Manatees?" asked Mel.

"No manatees," said their mother.

"Dugongs?"

"That's the same as manatees," said Lenny.

"No, it isn't," said Mel.

"Close enough," said their mother. "Animal Town helps injured animals. They live there until they get well. Like an animal nursing home."

"Are the animals all old?" asked Lenny.

"I bet they sit around in their pajamas all day and play bingo," said Mel.

"That's not what it's like at all," said their mother. "Everybody in the car."

The boys got up and slowly walked to the car.

They pulled into the gravel parking lot.

"Where are the animals' houses?" asked Lenny. "This doesn't look like a town at all."

"No, they're animals that live in the woods," said Mel. "They should live in campers."

"Manatees don't live in the woods," said Lenny.

"Neither do dugongs," said Mel.

"Knock it off, you two," said their mother. "Most of the animals here live in holes in the ground, not houses."

"Then they should call it 'A Bunch of Holes in the Ground with Animals in Them Town,'" said Lenny.

"It's more truthful," said Mel.

"I don't think that would fit on the sign," said their mother. "Now, let's go."

The boys and their mother walked up to a fenced-in area. FOX, said a sign on the fence.

"Where is he?" asked Mel.

"Probably in his hole," said their mother. "Foxes are nocturnal."

"Huh?" asked Lenny. He was only half-paying attention. Trying to see through the ground was tough business.

"Foxes only come out at night," said their mother. She made a face. "He sure is fragrant though."

"You bet," said Mel.

Just then a ranger walked up. "Hi, I'm Ranger Jorge," he said. "What do you guys think about the fox?"

"He reeks," said Lenny.

"Well, that's how he marks his territory," said Ranger Jorge.

"His territory reeks," said Mel.

"It keeps the other foxes away," said Ranger Jorge.

"Do you have any animals that come out during the day?" asked Lenny. "Or does the stinky fox keep them all away?"

"There's a squirrel over there," said Mel, pointing.

"The squirrels aren't part of Animal Town," said Ranger Jorge. "They just come and try to steal food from the residents."

"Even though they reek?" asked Lenny.

"Not all of them mark their territory like the fox does," said Ranger Jorge. "We've got an otter. He's usually out during the day."

"Maybe we otter see him," said Mel.

"If I had a nickel for every time I heard that," sighed Ranger Jorge.

"You'd probably have a quarter, I bet," said Lenny.

Ranger Jorge gave Lenny an odd look, and then he led them to the otter pen.

Two little eyes peered out of a murky puddle at the group.

"Is that it?" asked Mel.

"There's more to him, he's just underwater," said Ranger Jorge.

Suddenly the otter jumped out of the water and ran to the top of a dirt mound. He turned and slid on his stomach back down into the water. Then he peered back up at the group.

"Bravo!" said Mel.

"Right on!" said Lenny.

Lenny, Mel, and their mother clapped.

"Shhh," said Ranger Jorge. "Clapping upsets the animals. If you want to applaud, you have to clam-clap."

"Excuse me?" said Lenny.

Ranger Jorge held up one hand and slapped his fingers into his palm. "Clam-clap," he said.

"Clam-clap, eh?" said Mel.

The otter stayed put in the water. Otters don't care for clam-claps.

"Do you have a gift shop?" asked Lenny.

"Sure," said Ranger Jorge, disappointed that yet again the clam-clap was not a big success.

Lenny and Mel each got T-shirts that had an otter on them.

"They otter give those animals coffee or something so they stay awake during the day," said Lenny.

"We otter write a letter and suggest that," said Mel. Their mother sighed, knowing that they probably would.

JULY

Lunch Turkeys

July is sort of like June, but less exciting. After all, you've been doing this for a month now. Hot dogs are still plump, but not superplump. Wet dogs just smell okay, but not as bad as that fox in Animal Town. It still beats being in gym class.

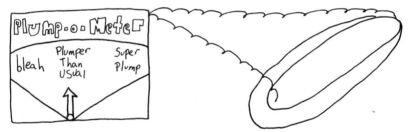

Plump-o-Meter

bleah | Plumper Than Usual | Super Plump

"I'm going to be out for a little while," said their mother. "You boys will have to make your own lunches."

"Okay," said Lenny.

"There's peanut butter in the cabinet, and jelly and bread in the refrigerator."

"Got it," said Mel.

They resumed their places in the living room.

"I don't want peanut butter," said Lenny.

"Me either," said Mel. "Let's see what else we have."

They went over to the refrigerator.

"Yikes!" said Lenny. "No wonder she suggested sandwiches. This place is empty."

"Is anything in there?" asked Mel.

"Well, bread and jelly," said Lenny. "Just like Mom said. That jar of pickle juice Dad said he was going to drink. Ugh, that vegetarian dog food Dad bought." He held up the can. "Dog Tofood."

"Tofood?" asked Mel.

"Yeah, it's got tofu in it," said Lenny.

"Oh. I thought you said 'toe food,'" said Mel. "Dogs will eat anything."

Lenny put the can of food down. "What's this?" He held up a tube of something.

"It says 'Pesto,'" said Mel. "It looks like toothpaste."

"I bet it's leftover toothpaste from when Mom and Dad went to Italy," said Lenny.

"Oh, yeah," said Mel. "Pesto, like toothpaste-o. I don't want to eat toothpaste for lunch though. What else is there?"

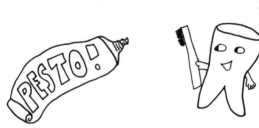

"Um, there's some bologna, and a couple of bowls of stuffing. They must be left over from Sunday's dinner."

"I wish we'd had potatoes instead of that stuffing," said Mel.

"Well," said Lenny, "we could make those things that they make at school where they wrap the big piece of turkey around the stuffing."

"Where are you getting this turkey?" asked Mel.

"Well, it's just lunch," said Lenny. "We don't need to be fancy and use real turkey. We can just use bologna."

"Is there turkey in bologna?" asked Mel.

"Beats me," said Lenny. "But it's all we've got."

"What about gravy?" asked Mel. "Lunch turkeys usually have gravy."

"We don't have any gravy," said Lenny. "Wait, ketchup is a kind of gravy, isn't it?"

"Well, it's gravier than nothing," said Mel.

They took the stuffing and the bologna and the ketchup and walked over to the table.

Lenny grabbed a handful of stuffing and began to make a ball.

"Wait," said Mel. "We need to use the proper equipment." He went over to the drawer where they kept the silverware and metal utensils. He rummaged around and pulled out a giant fork and a spatula that looked like it had been used a lot but never washed. Then finally he found what he was looking for. "The scoop!" he shouted, holding the ice-cream scoop over his head.

Lenny clam-clapped in approval.

Mel scooped out two perfect balls of stuffing,

giving a thumb flick that released the stuffing, and then a couple more just because he liked the sound it made. Lenny took a piece of bologna and wrapped it carefully around each stuffing blob. Then each boy added a squirt of ketchup to his creation. "Lunch turkeys are served," said Lenny.

They each cut a piece, tapped their forks together like they were doing a toast, and popped the pieces of lunch turkey into their mouths.

It was not what they had expected.

"This doesn't taste like the ones at school," said Lenny.

"This tastes like the dump," said Mel.

"Maybe we should have heated them up," said Lenny, trying to chew without tasting.

"Deep frying them might hide the flavor," said Mel.

"I don't want to have to taste them again if it doesn't work," said Lenny.

They both managed to swallow somehow.

"Where are we going to hide these?" asked Lenny.

"We could throw them at cars," said Mel.

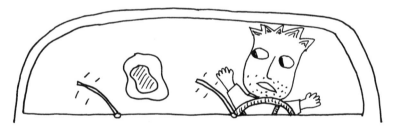

"I have a better idea," said Lenny.

"Did you guys make lunch okay?" asked their mother when she got home.

"Yes," said the boys.

"Why are your teeth green?" their mother asked.

"We used your Italian toothpaste after lunch," said Lenny.

"Italian toothpaste?" asked their mother. "Not the tube of pesto that was in there! That's not toothpaste, it's for putting on food."

"Oh," said Mel. "That might be why it wasn't so refreshing."

"Oh, no!" their mother shouted, looking out the window. "I think that pesky woodchuck has been out digging in my garden again! If he doesn't watch out, I'm going to send him to Animal Town."

"Oh, no," said Lenny.

"Oh no, indeed," said Mel. Then he whispered to Lenny, "If a lunch turkey tree grows out there, we're totally busted."

Their mother opened the refrigerator. "Oh, did you guys throw out that nasty old bowl of stuffing? I was worried your father was going to eat that thinking it was the stuff from Sunday."

Lenny and Mel looked at each other.

"Er, it's taken care of," said Lenny.

Pool Time

"I'm bored," said Lenny.

"Me too," said Mel.

"What should we do?" asked Lenny.

"I don't know," said Mel.

The dictionary was on the table. Their father had been using it for the crossword puzzle and hadn't put it away. Mel opened it.

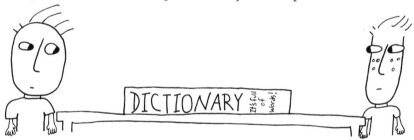

"What are you doing?" asked Lenny.

"Looking up 'boring'," said Mel. "'Boring: see bore. Bore: that which bores. See dullard.'" He looked at Lenny.

"Now what are you doing?" asked Lenny.

"Seeing a dullard," said Mel.

"If it weren't so hot, I'd come over and

get you," said Lenny. "Why does it have to be so hot?"

"That's what summer's all about," said Mel.

"Well, I can't take it anymore," said Lenny. "Let's see what we can do to cool off."

The boys walked into the kitchen. "Hey, Mom," said Lenny. "Can we get a pool?"

"Oh sure," said their mother. "We've got lots of money and a huge backyard for that."

"Fantastic," said Mel.

"I was joking," said their mother. "We don't have lots of money and our backyard is too small for a pool. Pools are big and expensive. Besides, they wouldn't come and build it today. You'd still be hot for a while."

"That stinks," said Lenny.

"You could go to the public pool," said their mother.

"Eek," said Mel. "Liquid cooties."

"I guess they don't do such a good job of keeping it clean, do they?" said their mother. "You could fill the tub with cold water and sit in there. That's sort of like a pool."

The boys went into the bathroom. Ahab was lying on his back in the tub with his legs sticking up in the air.

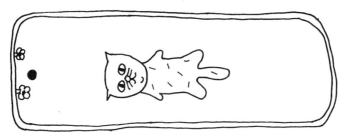

"Wow, it really is hot," said Mel. "Ahab only does that if it's super hot."

"Did you really need the cat to tell you it's hot?" asked Lenny.

"I'm just saying," said Mel.

"You're always just saying something," said
Lenny.

"Heat makes you cranky," said Mel.

"I know," said Lenny. "Let's get this tub
filled." Ahab put his ears back and gave them a
dirty look. "Or maybe not," said Lenny.

"We could make our own pool," said Mel.

"I'll call the cement truck," said Lenny.

"No, I've got a better way," said Mel.

The boys put on their swim trunks and
headed for the broom closet. "A trash bag for
you," said Mel, handing Lenny a trash bag,
"and a trash bag for me."

"What do I do with this?" asked Lenny.

"Come with me," said Mel.

They went out to the backyard. "Get in your bag," said Mel.

Lenny climbed in. Mel took the garden hose and stuck the end in the bag. "Now pull it, so just your head sticks out," he said to Lenny. Lenny pulled the bag shut. Mel turned on the hose.

"EEEEEEEEEEEEEEEEEEEEEGAAAAAAA AAAAAAAAAAAAAH!" shouted Lenny. "That's freezing."

"Well, you're not hot anymore, are you?" said Mel.

"No," said Lenny, "but still, eeeeeeeeeeee-gaaaaaaaaaaaaah!"

When Lenny's bag was full, Mel pulled the hose out. Then he got into his own bag, put the hose in, and pulled the top tight. "I see what you mean with the eegah," he said to Lenny.

"How are you going to get the hose out?" asked Lenny.

"I have no idea," said Mel. He hoped he'd cool off before his bag burst.

Summer Reading

"Do you guys have any summer reading to do this year?" asked the boys' mother.

"We did it already," said Lenny.

"Do you have to give a book report?" asked their mother.

"We did those, too," said Mel.

"Wow," said their mother. "You're really ahead of yourselves this year. Why don't you give your reports to me later on today? A little practice never hurt anyone."

"Fine with me," said Lenny.

In the living room they set up a little fake classroom. They used TV trays for desks.

Lenny and Mel each had their own desk, and their mother had one set up at the front of the room the way a teacher would.

"Lenny, why don't you go first?" their mother said.

Mel had been about to pass a note to him that said, "The teacher smells." Lenny quickly acted like nothing was happening and walked to the front of the room. He cleared his throat.

"My book report," he said. "Termites live in groups called colonies. They have a queen.

They like to eat wood. Some of them have wings, but some of them don't. Sometimes you will see termite wings in your home. If you do, this is not good. If you see this, then you need to call Termite Man. He can take care of your termite needs at a price you can afford."

Mel clam-clapped politely.

"Any questions?" Lenny asked.

Mel raised his hand, but their mother butted in. "Just what was the name of this book?" she asked.

"*How to Tell if You Have Termites,*" said Lenny.

"And where did you get this book?"

"The hardware store."

"I see. Mel, what book did you read?"

"*The Many Faces of Pimples,*" said Mel.

"And where did your book come from?" she asked.

"The drugstore," he said.

"Boys, I hate to tell you this, but you can't use advertising pamphlets for your summer reading books."

"We just wanted something we could read quickly, so we didn't have to spend all summer working on our reports," said Mel.

"Well, that's fine," said their mother, "but you're going to have to read something a little longer than one page. Get in the car, we're going to the library."

The boys got to the library and wandered around the shelves.

"What do you want to read about?" Lenny asked Mel.

"I don't know," said Mel. "Apes?"

"Apes are good," said Lenny. "Dogs too."

They searched through the animal section until they found a couple of books that didn't seem like they'd be too painful to read. As they went up to the counter to check them out they heard their mother call them.

"Boys, come over here. There are some people I want you to meet."

Lenny and Mel walked over.

"I'd like you to meet the parents of one of your classmates," she said. "These are the Bunkleheimers."

The boys gasped. If Art's parents were there, Art might not be far behind. And he wasn't.

"Oh, it's you two," Art said, appearing from behind a shelf of romance novels, sneering. The boys sneered back. None of the parents seemed to notice.

"Do you smell cake?" asked Lenny.

"Oh, that's me," said Mrs. Bunkleheimer.

 "I work in a bakery. I have a hard time getting the smell off me, so I gave up trying to fight it."

"And what do you do?" the boys' mother asked Mr. Bunkleheimer.

"I'm a doctor," he said.

"What kind?" asked Mel.

"A podiatrist," said Mr. Bunkleheimer.

"When you come home from work, do you smell like feet?" asked Lenny. The boys giggled.

"Just my hands," he said.

The boys stopped giggling and would have yelled "eegah!" if they hadn't been in the library. "We're going to go check out our books," said Lenny, and he and Mel ran off to the circulation desk.

"Man, running into people you know during vacation is the worst," said Lenny.

"I know," said Mel. "Don't they know they're supposed to stay away?"

"That settles it," said Lenny. "No more leaving the house for the rest of the summer. We can't take that kind of risk."

"If we were at camp, we'd be surrounded by Bunkleheimer types," said Mel.

"Don't remind me," said Lenny.

"Like that time they tied you to the seesaw and kept jumping off the other end so you'd smack into the ground," Mel continued.

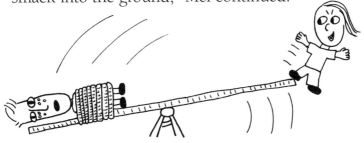

"I said don't remind me," said Lenny.

"I was reminding myself," said Mel.

A Grand Adventure

August, in spite of family vacations, is a good month. You'd think you'd be bored of summer by now. Nope. You've only got a month left, so you've got to make the most of it. Even a bad vacation is better than no vacation.

"It is now August," the boys' father announced. "That means it's time to go to the cabin!"

Mel pushed Valentine off his face and looked at the clock. "It's four thirty in the morning," he said.

"Fnama homina," said Lenny, rolling over.

"What a couple of duds," said their father. "Awaken!" he shouted.

The only one who listened was Valentine, who began to lick Mel's face.

"Auuuugh! Dog drool!" shouted Mel. "I'm up! I'm up!" He leapt out of bed, wiping his face wildly.

Valentine jumped onto Lenny's bed. He licked and licked Lenny's face, but Lenny didn't budge. "I'm delicious," he said after a little while, and then rolled over. Valentine stopped licking and curled up next to him.

"Hey, knock it off," said their father, shooing Valentine out of the bed. He picked up Lenny and carried him out to the kitchen.

Their mother was there, looking very tired. "Why so early?" she mumbled. "Why always so early?"

"Well, we've got to beat the traffic," said their father. "Plus, we have to pick up Grandma."

"I bet Grandma is still asleep," said their mother.

"So is Lenny," said Mel, and he kicked Lenny's chair.

"Oklahoma!" shouted Lenny, snapping awake. "Hey, where's the wagon train?" he asked.

"Right here!" said their father.

"Trust me, you were dreaming," said Mel.

"I loaded the luggage last night, so we can get going right away," said their father.

"Hurrah," said a very dejected family.

Once they finished their breakfast, the family walked out to the car. Well, first Lenny and Mel tried to head for their spots in the living room. "Get in the car, you two," snapped their mother. The boys quickly changed their course and headed for the garage.

They were greeted by an impressive sight.

Their father had stacked up their suitcases
on the roof of their tiny car and tied them
down. It looked like an Egyptian pyramid.
Except that it was made of fake leather. And
covered in flower stickers, so no one would
steal them at the airport.

"What if they fall down?" asked Mel.

"Oh, they won't," said their father. "I spent
a few hours getting this ready last night. It's all
done perfectly."

"Why can't I open the door?" asked Lenny.

"Did you tie the doors shut?" asked their
mother.

"Uh . . . ," said their father.

"How do we get in?" asked Mel.

"Well, I can't undo it after all that work," said their father. "Everyone in the windows."

The boys climbed right in. Their mother shot their father a dirty look, and then climbed in. Finally their father climbed in, and they were off.

"To Grandma's!" he shouted.

When they pulled up to Grandma's house, she was sitting on a suitcase on her front steps, sound asleep. Their father beeped the horn.

Grandma jumped up and started yelling, "Scare an old lady to death, why don't you?"

"Hey, no sleeping," said their father. "We're on vacation."

"On my vacations I like to sleep," said Grandma. "Like normal people. If we didn't leave so early, I could have done it right." She looked at the car. "Did you tie the doors shut?"

"Um . . . ," said their father.

"Well, everyone out of my way if I've got to climb in," she said. "Lenny and Mel, you sit on my suitcase," she said, stuffing it through the window. She climbed over the boys' father and into the backseat.

"This suitcase is awful full, Grandma," said Lenny.

"I need my vacation hats," said Grandma.

"How many vacation hats do you have in there?" asked Mel.

"Well," said Grandma. "I've got my beach hat, for the beach. I've got my walking hat, for walking around. I've got a baseball hat, but I really only wear that when I play Frisbee. I've got my beekeeping hat, just in case. I've got a rubber werewolf mask, also just in case. There may be some others in there I don't remember. I keep the suitcase packed at all times. You never know when you may need to run off on vacation."

"I didn't realize this stuff was so complicated," said Lenny.

"Me neither," said Mel. "We didn't even bring sitting-around hats."

"You do a good enough job without hats," said their father. "Now, away we go!"

The Drive

The drive to get on vacation is never short.
And when you're sitting on a suitcase full of
old lady hats, it can really make the time drag.

"Are we there yet?" asked Mel.

"Yes," said their father. "We've been there
awhile. I'm just driving around to use up the
rest of the gas."

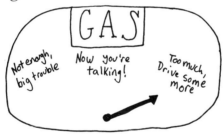

"That seems wasteful," said Mel.

"I was joking," said their father. "We've still
got a ways to go."

"Why does getting to vacation take so
long?" asked Lenny.

"Because you have to get up so early,"
whispered Grandma.

"Well, you want to go far away from where you are normally," said their father. "Otherwise you might as well just sit around the house."

"We've been doing that all summer," said Mel. "Why stop now?"

"You'll get bored soon enough," said their father.

"Nonsense," said Grandma. "Nothing beats doing nothing all day. Anyone who tells you differently is a nuthead."

"Well, it's still going to be awhile," said their mother. "Why don't you play a game?"

Mel looked out the window. They passed a sign that said, DO NOT PASS.

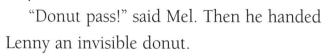

"Donut pass!" said Mel. Then he handed Lenny an invisible donut.

Lenny pretended to eat it. "Mmmm, chocolate cruller," he said.

They drove for a little while longer. Eventually another DO NOT PASS sign went by. "Donut pass!" shouted Lenny, and he handed Mel an invisible donut.

"Mmmm, barbarian creme," said Mel.

"Don't you mean Bavarian creme?" asked their mother.

"Nope," said Mel. "You should taste this thing. Want a bite?" He handed it to his mother.

"Er, no thank you," said their mother.

A little while later they passed another sign. "Donut pass!" shouted Grandma. She handed Lenny an invisible donut.

"Hey, what flavor is this?" asked Lenny, taking a bite.

"Hedgehog," said Grandma.

"Ooh, spiny," said Mel.

"Bleah," said Lenny, spitting out an invisible chunk of donut. "I don't think I want to play this game anymore."

"Well, boys," said Grandma, "if we're not playing any games, the only way to make a trip like this go by fast is to zonk out. See you when we get there." And with that, she shut her eyes and quickly fell asleep.

"Man, Grandma knows everything," said Lenny.

"You know it," said Mel. And then they both shut their eyes and zonked out.

The Cabin

"Wake up, everyone, we're here!" shouted their father.

The boys woke up and looked at a cabin that could have fit in their garage.

"Is this the toolshed?" asked Lenny.

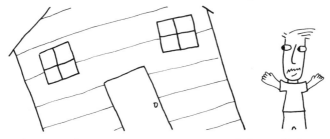

"This is where we're staying," said their father.

"We're staying in a toolshed?" asked Mel.

"No, this is a vacation cabin," said their father.

"Don't people stay in houses for vacation?" asked Lenny.

"They could, I suppose," said their father. "But if you live in a house anyway, where's the change?"

"Well, if you stay in a toolshed, where's

the comfort?" asked Grandma.

"Well, this is where we're staying, so everyone get used to it," said their father.

Everybody went inside. The cabin was pretty much one room, part of it a living room with three couches, a smaller part that was a kitchen, and then a tiny bathroom.

"Where are the beds?" asked Mel, looking at the couches.

"The couches fold out into beds," said their father. "They just keep them as couches to save space. Watch." He folded one of the couches out into a bed. "See?" he said.

"How are the other ones going to fold out?" asked Grandma. "Are we supposed to sleep on top of each other?"

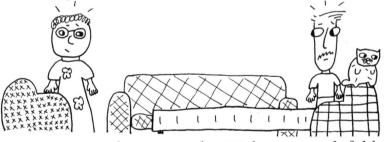

Grandma was right. With one couch folded out, the other two would have to fold out right on top of it.

"Well, I guess we'll have to take turns having our couches fold out," said their father. "Grandma can go first."

"You'd better believe it," said Grandma, climbing onto the folded-out couch and getting comfortable.

"Hey, our couch smells like feet," said Lenny.

"Yikes. I wonder if Mr. Bunkleheimer slept on it," said Mel.

"Bleah, Dr. Foothands," said Lenny.

"This one smells like a pizza," said their mother. Valentine had camped out in front of the pizza couch with his nose pressed into the fabric.

"Think of it as an adventure," said their father.

"Why are adventures always something bad?" asked Mel.

"That's how parents keep you from complaining," said Grandma. "My couch smells like a home perm. Let's go get some fresh air."

Hot Dog Time

"Hey, everyone," shouted their father. "It's cookout time."

"Somebody better wake up Grandma," said Lenny.

"Where is she?" asked their mother.

"Out back, sleeping under a tree," said Mel. "She said she doesn't like the way the couches smell."

"Valentine does," said Lenny. "He won't stop licking the pizza one."

"I'll get Grandma," said their mother. "You boys go get the hot dogs."

Lenny went to the refrigerator. There was one package marked FRANKS and one marked WEINERS.

"Which one should I grab?" he asked Mel.

"I don't know," said Mel. "What's the difference?"

"Let's ask Dad," said Lenny. He grabbed both packages, and the boys walked out to the grill.

"Hey, Dad," Lenny said, "what's the difference between franks and weiners?"

"Which ones are hot dogs?" asked Mel.

"Well, they're all hot dogs," he said. "I don't know the difference, though. Let me see the packages." He looked closely at each of them. "I think they have different ingredients."

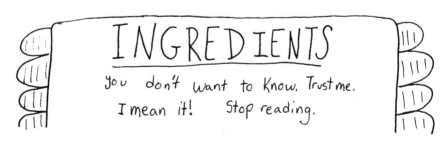

INGREDIENTS

you don't want to know. Trust me.
I mean it! Stop reading.

"Oh," said Mel. "Like hot dogs are made of hamburger, but weiners are made of fruit and mice."

"You're thinking of cider," said their father.

Grandma wandered over wearing a baseball hat.

"How come you're wearing your Frisbee hat?" asked Mel.

"I think I've been wearing too many hats," said Grandma.

"What do you mean?" asked Lenny.

Grandma took off her hat, and she was completely bald, except for a little hair on the sides of her head, and a few strands she combed over the top.

"AAAAH!" shouted Lenny and Mel.

"Just kidding," said Grandma. "It's a wig."

"Phew," said Mel.

"You really do have everything in that suitcase," said Lenny.

"What's so great about cookouts?" asked Lenny.

"We're eating outside," said Mel.

"Whoopee," said Lenny.

"If you'd gone to camp, you would have gotten to eat outside every day," said their father.

"Yeah, but we'd also get french fries thrown at us," said Mel.

"Then Mel would get mad and go hide in the tire swing," said Lenny.

"That's how I got the tire swing crud on my pants," said Mel.

"I remember that," said their mother. "I had to throw those pants away."

"At least the couches smell better than that," said Lenny.

"Well, no one's going to throw french fries at you here," said their father. "Grandma! Stop that!"

Grandma hid the french fry behind her back. "What? I wasn't doing anything," she said.

The End

"Are you boys packed and ready to go tomorrow?" asked their mother.

"Yes," said the boys.

"Just think, when we get back, there'll only be two days until school starts."

"Don't remind me," said Lenny.

"We'll have to go and get you some new school clothes when we get back," said their mother.

"No fair!" said Mel. "We can't use a vacation day for shopping."

"We're almost all out!" said Lenny.

"Can't we do it on a school day?" asked Mel.

"No, you're supposed to be in school on school days," said their mother.

"But if we're doing school business, doesn't that count?" asked Lenny.

"No," said their mother.

"Why do we need new clothes anyway?" asked Mel. "Why can't we just keep wearing the old ones?"

"You need new clothes to look nice," said their mother.

"We didn't look nice before?" asked Lenny. "Why'd you buy us those clothes if we didn't look nice?"

"It's all a scam," said Grandma. "She was trying to make everyone think you were hobos."

"That's not true at all," said their mother. "When your clothes were new last year, they were nice. Now we're used to them, so we get new ones that will be nice for a while."

"Until we get used to them," said Grandma.

"Anyway, you can't go to school without nice new school clothes," said their mother, "and that's final."

"We can't, eh?" said Lenny. He looked at Mel. "I bet we can think of something," he whispered.

The boys nodded at each other. Two days was plenty of time.

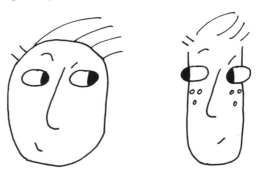